* chicken tempo

CUNNINGHAM'S ROOSTER

Story by Barbara Brenner   Pictures by Anne Rockwell

Parents' Magazine Press / New York

Library of Congress Cataloging in Publication Data
Brenner, Barbara.
    Cunningham's rooster.
    SUMMARY: Cunningham, the song-writing cat, acquires a
rooster who gives him inspiration for even greater songs,
including his masterpiece.
    [1. Music — Fiction] I. Rockwell, Anne F., illus.
II. Title.
PZ7.B7518Cu [E] 74-12285
ISBN 0-8193-0783-1
ISBN 0-8193-0784-X (lib. bdg.)

for Arthur and all the cats
who make music

There was once a cat named Cunningham who made music. That was his work. He made up songs for singing and songs for dancing and music just for listening.

First he would hear a song in his head. Then he would play it on the piano. After a while he would write the notes down in his big black notebook with a felt pen, so he wouldn't forget how the tune went.

They were fine songs, too. The only trouble was, nobody heard them. Because Cunningham lived all alone except for his goldfish. And everyone knows that a goldfish has no ear for music.

It was beginning to get Cunningham down.
"What good is a song if there's no one to hear it?"
he asked himself.

One day as he sat playing the piano and wishing that a goldfish *did* have an ear for music, there was a pecking sound at the sliding glass door. He looked up to see who it was.

It was a rooster.

"My name is Kenneth," the rooster announced, pushing open the door with his beak. "I was passing by. I stopped to tell you that I really like that song you're playing. It's mellow."

Cunningham couldn't have been more pleased.

"There's more where that came from," he said. "Why don't you step inside?"

Kenneth did, and Cunningham played him every song he had ever made up. Songs for singing and songs for dancing and melodies that were just for listening. When the music was all over, Kenneth flapped his wings and clucked with pleasure.

Cunningham knew then that he and the rooster were in perfect harmony.

"Stay with me," he urged Kenneth. "You can be
the first one to hear my new songs. You'll give me
Inspiration."

"What is Inspiration?" Kenneth wanted to know.

"It's the feeling a cat gets that makes him hear songs in his head," Cunningham explained.

"Well," said Kenneth, "I'll certainly try to give you some. What will you give me?"

"A roost of your own and all the brown rice you can eat."

"It's a deal," said Kenneth promptly. He picked out a roost in Cunningham's bookcase and went to sleep, thinking how lucky he was not to be in the crowded barnyard anymore.

Having someone to listen to his music changed Cunningham's life. Now every day found him happily at work, making up songs and then writing them down in his big black notebook.

As for Kenneth, every day found him sitting under the piano listening to Cunningham's songs. Or sitting on the piano watching Cunningham write down notes. Or scratching around out in the yard talking in riddles to the bugs before he ate them.

"Do bugs look like notes of music or do notes of music look like bugs?" That was a question Kenneth never tired of asking.

One day Cunningham was watching Kenneth out in the yard. Suddenly he said, "I have an Inspiration. I will make up some music about Kenneth. It will be a musical poem—a *rhapsody!* It will have three parts to it. And I will call it the *Rooster Rhapsody!*"

He sat right down at the piano and began.

The first part was all about Kenneth. It was about how Kenneth looked and the things Kenneth did and what Kenneth was like. There were soft sounds in it—like the clucking sounds that Kenneth made when he talked to bugs. And there were trills like Kenneth's wattles shaking when he walked. And there was a little strutty dance that was Kenneth when he scratched in the dirt. Altogether it was a wonderful song, as light as feathers and as happy as a rooster crowing in the morning.

When Kenneth heard the music, he loved it.

"It's me all over!" he said.

Cunningham was pleased, too. He thought it was by far the best thing he had ever made up. He decided to take it down to the city and show it to an Important Music Person.

Before he left, Cunningham filled Kenneth's dish with brown rice and had a serious talk with him.

"Kenneth," he said, "there is a hungry opossum who lives back in the woods. She has fifty teeth and likes nothing better than to eat plump chickens. So promise me that you won't go out into the yard after dark."

Kenneth promised.

All went well during the day. But toward evening, moths began to gather on the screens. The fireflies winked at Kenneth from outside. The moon rose and made the trees look like shadows and the shadows look like trees.

Kenneth began to feel restless. He longed to talk in riddles to the fireflies. And he wanted to visit his old barnyard friends.

At last Kenneth said, "This is the sort of night when a rooster could break a promise."

He slid the glass door open with his beak and stepped out into the darkness.

He clucked softly to a firefly. "Is a bug like a note of music or is a note of music like…"

But before Kenneth had even gotten to the end
of his riddle, the hungry opossum crept quietly out
of the shadows and…*pounced!*

Cunningham came home feeling cheerful. The Important Music Person liked his work. He said he wouldn't be at all surprised if the *Rooster Rhapsody* made Cunningham famous. Cunningham couldn't wait to tell Kenneth.

But Kenneth was nowhere to be found.

Cunningham went to the kitchen. The brown rice was there but Kenneth wasn't. And he wasn't roosting in the bookcase or under the piano or in any of his usual places.

Finally Cunningham took a lantern and went out to the backyard. There on the ground were the tracks of an opossum and four golden feathers from a rooster's tail.

It didn't take long for Cunningham to guess what had happened.

It was a sad cat who walked back into the house
that night.

He sat down at the piano. He thought of all the fine times that were over, and all the sad years ahead.

Slowly, Cunningham began to make up a new song. It was a song as restless as a spring night and as mysterious as shadows. Some of it sounded like an animal pouncing, and some of it was slow and low and full of the sadness of losing a friend.

"This is the second part of my *Rooster Rhapsody*," said Cunningham with tears in his eyes. "But it is the last song I will ever make up. My Inspiration is gone. And what is a musician without his Inspiration?" he asked himself. "What is a cat without his work?"

He closed up the piano. He put away the big
black notebook and put the cap on the felt pen.
Then Cunningham lay down in his bed and pulled
the covers over his head.

The days passed. The milk got sour on the back porch. The dust collected on the piano. Algae began to form in the goldfish bowl.

Then one morning there was a tapping at the sliding glass door.

"Come in," called Cunningham weakly, not even bothering to open his eyes.

A few moments later he heard a scratching sound. The next thing he knew, someone was pulling the covers from his head.

Cunningham opened one eye. It was Kenneth!

"Dear friend," cried Cunningham, "is it really you?"

"No one else but," clucked Kenneth reassuringly.

"I thought you'd been gobbled!" said Cunningham. "There were tracks of opossum. And there were rooster feathers…"

"Tut-tut, old friend," said Kenneth soothingly. "No harm done. Remember...an opossum can pounce, but a rooster can roost! That's what I did. Went up a tree for safety. Nothing lost except a few tail feathers."

"But why didn't you come back sooner?"

"I should have," Kenneth admitted. "But it was such a lovely spring night, and I wanted to visit some old friends in the barnyard."

Cunningham didn't have the heart to be angry with Kenneth. Also, at that moment, a new song came into his head. He opened the piano and began to play.

What a song it was! A joyful song, full of mellow chords and notes that were as golden as Kenneth's tail. It was a song about a friend's coming back and the happiness that comes with him. It was a song for everyone in the world and for every instrument in the orchestra.

Now the three parts of the *Rooster Rhapsody* were finished. After Cunningham wrote down the last notes, he played the whole thing straight through...

He played the first part, which was light as a feather.

And the second part, which was slow and sad and low.

And he played the last part, which was mellow and golden.

Each song by itself was fine. But all together they made the most magical music ever.

All the animals came out of the woods to hear the *Rooster Rhapsody*. The birds came, and the squirrels, and the rabbits and the raccoons. Even the deer came. Soon the whole backyard was filled with animals. And every animal who heard that music went away happier.

As for Kenneth, he almost burst with pride.
He threw back his head and crowed for joy. Cunningham wrote down the sounds of Kenneth's crowing, and they became the final notes of the *Rooster Rhapsody*.

The rhapsody *did* make Cunningham famous. It made Kenneth famous, too. Whenever the *Rooster Rhapsody* was played, someone would ask who had been the inspiration for such wonderful music. Then someone else would always remember, and tell the story of Cunningham's rooster.

Fowl Strut

ARTHUR CUNNINGHAM

Rooster Rhapsody